Ruby's Falling Leaves

Based on the characters created by Rosemary Wells

Grosset & Dunlap

GROSSET & DUNLAP
Published by the Penguin Group
Penguin Group (USA) Inc., 375 Hudson Street, New York, New York 10014, U.S.A.
Penguin Group (Canada), 90 Eglinton Avenue East, Suite 700, Toronto, Ontario, Canada M4P 2Y3
(a division of Pearson Penguin Canada Inc.)
Penguin Books Ltd, 80 Strand, London WC2R 0RL, England
Penguin Ireland, 25 St Stephen's Green, Dublin 2, Ireland
(a division of Penguin Books Ltd)
Penguin Group (Australia), 250 Camberwell Road, Camberwell, Victoria 3124, Australia
(a division of Pearson Australia Group Pty Ltd)
Penguin Books India Pvt Ltd, 11 Community Centre, Panchsheel Park, New Delhi - 110 017, India
Penguin Group (NZ), 67 Apollo Drive, Mairangi Bay, Auckland 1311, New Zealand
(a division of Pearson New Zealand Ltd.)
Penguin Books (South Africa) (Pty) Ltd, 24 Sturdee Avenue, Rosebank, Johannesburg 2196, South Africa

Penguin Books Ltd, Registered Offices:
80 Strand, London WC2R 0RL, England

Based upon the animated series *Max & Ruby*
A Nelvana Limited production © 2002–2003.

Max & Ruby ™ and © Rosemary Wells. NELVANA™ Nelvana Limited. CORUS™ Corus Entertainment Inc.

All Rights Reserved. Used under license by Penguin Young Readers Group.

Published in 2007 by Grosset & Dunlap, a division of Penguin Young Readers Group, 345 Hudson Street, New York, New York 10014.

GROSSET & DUNLAP is a trademark of Penguin Group (USA) Inc. Printed in the U.S.A.

Library of Congress Control Number: 2007004330

ISBN 978-0-448-44686-8   10 9 8 7 6 5 4 3 2

"Summer is over, Max," said Max's sister, Ruby.
"Now it's fall!"
"Fall!" said Max.

"Yes, Max," said Ruby. "It's called fall because all
the leaves fall down from the trees."

4

"Down!" said Max.

"I have to make a leaf collection for school, Max,"
said Ruby. "You can help me find the leaves."

6

"Up!" said Max, pointing to the trees.
"No, Max," said Ruby. "We want the leaves that are down on the ground."

7

"Look, Max," said Ruby. "I've already found ten elm leaves, three birch leaves, and four different oak leaves!"

Ruby put all the leaves in her leaf book.

8

"Next I need to find leaves from a willow tree and an apple tree," said Ruby.

Max found more leaves.

"Down!" said Max as he put the leaves on the pile.

"Perfect, Max! Here's an apple tree leaf.
And here's a willow tree leaf!" said Ruby.

10

"Now all I need is a Japanese maple leaf and a big tooth aspen," said Ruby. "I'm not stopping until I find them all."

Right in the middle of Max's dump truck was a big red leaf.

"Wow!" said Ruby. "A Japanese maple leaf."

"Up and over!" said Max as he emptied his dump truck.
"Oh no, Max," said Ruby.
The big red maple leaf went right into Ruby's leaf pile.

"How will I ever find that maple leaf?" asked Ruby.

But Max found the leaf for her.
Ruby put the red maple leaf into her book.

15

"Now I just have to find a big tooth aspen leaf,"
Ruby said.

16

Ruby spotted an orange leaf on the very top of a tree.
"Look, Max!" said Ruby. "A big tooth aspen leaf."
"Up!" said Max.
The wind blew the leaf off the tree.
"Down!" said Max.

The aspen leaf landed in Max's wheelbarrow.
"Down!" said Max as he dumped the wheelbarrow over.
"Now we'll never find it, Max!" exclaimed Ruby.

Ruby swished through all the leaves.
"My book won't be finished without the aspen leaf, Max," said Ruby.

19

"Don't move, Max!" said Ruby. "I think I see the aspen leaf."

"Here it is, Max!" said Ruby.

Ruby checked her book, but this leaf was from an oak, not an aspen.

"Well," said Ruby, "I guess I will have an empty page in my book."

Just then, Max jumped into the leaf pile!

Then he threw the leaves up in the air!

Suddenly an orange leaf floated toward Ruby. "Max!" cried Ruby as she caught the leaf. "It's my aspen leaf! How did you find it?" "Fall!" said Max.